This Book Belongs to:

_____

It Was Given to Me by:

_____

On This Date:

_____

THE BIBLE AMIGOS
JONAH AND THE BEAR

THE BIBLE AMIGOS
JONAH AND THE BEAR

Written and Illustrated by

Frank Fraser

SHILOH kidz

An Imprint of Barbour Publishing, Inc.

ISBN 978-1-62416-887-1

Published in association with the Blythe Daniel Agency, Inc., P.O. Box 64197, Colorado Springs CO 80962.

Published by Shiloh Kidz, an imprint of Barbour Publishing, Inc., P.O. Box 719, Uhrichsville, Ohio 44683, www.shilohkidz.com

Our mission is to publish and distribute inspirational products offering exceptional value and biblical encouragement to the masses.

Member of the
Evangelical Christian
Publishers Association

Printed in China.
04728 1014 SC

For the person who encouraged me to write it: Jesus.
He has been my biggest fan for a really long time.
Thank You for always loving my work, even when it wasn't
very good. Thank You for always believing in me.
I will do my very best to always believe in You.

For my wife, without whom I would have never heard
God's quiet invitation to write and illustrate books for Him.

For all the Bible Amigos around the world.
Keep searching, praying, and loving.

Edge and Walla were finishing up their chores when they heard a terrible sound. *Bumpity-bumpity. . . Bumpity-bumpity. . .*

"What's that?" Walla said, afraid to turn around.

"I don't know. But whatever it is, it sounds mad. And it's coming right at us!" cried Edge.

Bumpity-bumpity. . . Bumpity-bumpity. . . BUMP!

"Donk! It's just you!" said Walla.

"Yep. It's just dizzy, bumpy me! The sack got so heavy with the harvest I couldn't carry it, so I rolled down in it! Ouch!" He rubbed his head. "I won't do *that* again. But just look at what God gave us today!"

Walla agreed. "God is awesome—He gives us so much."

"I just wish He didn't give us so many leaves!" grumbled Edge.

Suddenly, a mighty wind picked up the whole pile of leaves and dumped them on Edge's head.

"You know what that wind means?" asked Walla.

"More leaves to rake?" groaned Edge.

"No, silly," said Walla. "There's the answer I was looking for!"

A big Bible came swooping down on the mighty wind, like a graceful bird, landing in front of their home as it usually did.

Walla was the first to hop on. "C'mon Bible Amigos! I wonder who needs our help this time!"

Then Donk climbed aboard. "I wonder where this next adventure will take us."

Edge climbed on last, grumbling to himself. "And I wonder: Will there be trees with leaves?"

As the wind lifted the Bible, the Bible Amigos cheered. . .

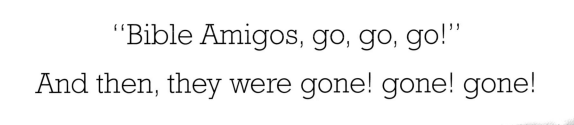

"Bible Amigos, go, go, go!"

And then, they were gone! gone! gone!

Meanwhile, over the hills, across the ocean, past the shiny city, around the block, on the front lawn of Mr. and Mrs. Bear, a storm was kicking up—

I WANT SOMETHING NEW!

and its name was Bear Junior. . .

Although Bear Junior was surrounded with all kinds of fun things to play with—bouncy things, noisy things, funny things, and wiggly things—he didn't want to play with any of them. He wanted something new. But little did he know that something new *was* coming. And this new something was not the kind of new that he had wished for.

This new something was new neighbors across the street. Some of them were bouncy, some were noisy, some were funny, and a couple were wiggly! Bear Junior noticed them looking at him and his toys. And then, one of them waved.

"Uh-oh," thought Bear Junior. "I think they want me to share *my* toys!"

Bear Junior was about to do something not very nice, until he remembered what his mom always said: "God asks us to be generous and ready to share."

So, taking a deep breath, he gathered all his toys into his arms, and. . .

...he ran away!

He ran down the trail toward the pond. And when he got to the end of the trail, Bear Junior jumped into a little boat. He loaded it with his toys, and then he climbed to the top of his tower of stuff.

This bear was *not* going to share.

From his shaky perch, he watched out for the new neighbors until. . .he spied a giant flying Bible landing in the nearby field!

The three Bible Amigos jumped off. Walla and Edge went one way while Donk followed the trail that ended at the dock right by the little boat.

"Who are you? What are you doing?" yelled Bear Junior from his lofty perch. "You can't have my toys!"

"I don't want your toys," said Donk. "I'm looking for someone. Maybe you can see them from up there? Would you mind taking a look around?"

"I guess I could. What do they look like?" asked Bear Junior.

"I'm not sure." Donk gave it some serious thought. Then, after a moment, he said. "I think they probably look like they're in trouble!"

"In trouble, huh? Well, all right. Let me look." Bear Junior tried to look around, but whenever he moved the tower swayed. He thought, *"If this keeps swaying I might fall off, and I can't swim!"* The idea of it scared him. He had a sinking feeling that this was not a good idea to be up so high.

While Bear Junior looked, Donk noticed something. "Hey, there's a little boat down there."

"Yes, I know," grumbled Bear Junior.

Donk asked, "Isn't a boat supposed to float?"

"Well, of course a boat is supposed to float," Bear Junior snapped.

"That's what I thought," said Donk. "But maybe you put too much in your boat, because now your boat is sinking!"

HELP!

"What? Oh no!" cried Bear Junior. "If the boat can't float, and I can't swim, then I'm in trouble!"

Walla and Edge came running when they heard Bear Junior shout for help "Donk, you found him—the one we came to help."

"I did? Oh yes, I did!" Donk grinned proudly.

Edge said to Bear Junior, "So, how did you get yourself up there on a shaky stack in a sinking boat?" After Bear Junior told them the whole story, Edge said, "So you're a bear that won't share, in a boat that won't float?"

"Yes, I am," Bear Junior sighed. "Can you help me?"

"We sure can!" Walla ran to the big Bible and gave it a big hug. "With this—the Bible, the Word of God. When you read it, the words come to life and show you the way God wants you to live."

"And also the way out of trouble?" asked Bear Junior, hopefully.

"That, too!" said Donk as he and Edge began turning the Bible's giant pages.

Flip, flip, flip. Page after page they turned. And then. . .

"Whoa! This must be it!" Walla said. "Thank you, Bible, we'll take it from here."
Then she said, "Donk, turn the page. Let's see what God wants to tell a bear
who won't share.

"A long time ago. . ."

Jonah 1, 2, 3:1-3

". . .God asked a man named Jonah to take a message to people in another town. Jonah said, 'Sure God,' but he didn't really mean it. Jonah didn't want to do what God asked.

"As soon as Jonah thought God had left him, he jumped onto a boat to get away from God."

"Uh-oh," Bear Junior thought out loud. "This already sounds familiar."

To Nineveh

"But God is always with us," Edge continued. "Even if we can't see Him. So, of course, God saw Jonah trying to run away."

"Then what happened?" asked Bear Junior. (He was almost afraid to know.)

"God made a big storm on the ocean, and Jonah wound up getting tossed over the side of the boat! He couldn't swim, and he began to sink—

But God loved Jonah. So he sent a great whale to save him. And with ONE. . .BIG. . .GULP. . .the whale swallowed Jonah up! Jonah slipped down into the whale's belly where it was dark, and he was all alone."

"Was he afraid?" Bear Junior asked.

"Of course he was afraid! And Jonah's thoughts drifted to what God had asked him to do. He realized it was wrong of him not to do what God had asked. So Jonah said to God, 'I'm sorry, God. I know You love me, and You only ask me to do things that are good.' And that must have made God very happy because—*whoosh!*—"

"That whale blasted Jonah back onto dry land!"

"God gave Jonah a second chance, and this time Jonah thanked God and took the message to the people in the other town. From that day on, Jonah always did what God asked."

"The End."

"That's a great story," Bear Junior said. "*But I'm still sinking!*"

"Remember," said Walla. "The Bible isn't just a story, it's the Word of God. It's how He talks to us and tells us what we need to do."

Bear Junior thought about that. It didn't take him long to realize he was like Jonah. "God asks us to be generous and ready to share," he thought out loud. "I didn't do what God asked. Maybe God was talking to me through Jonah's story."

Bear Junior looked across the pond and saw his new neighbors. He felt sorry for the way he had treated them, but mostly he felt sorry for how he had treated God.

So, having learned a lesson from Jonah, Bear Junior prayed. "God, I'm really, really sorry. I should have shared like You asked me to. I'll try to do whatever You ask from now on."

And no sooner had Bear Junior finished his prayer than he and all of his toys were—*whoosh!*—blown out of the pond by a whale!

Saved from the sinking boat, Bear Junior thanked God. Then he called his new neighbors over to play with his toys. As Bear Junior and his new friends played, he noticed that he was actually *happy* to share his things. Doing what God asked made him feel good.

Reaching into his toy pile for another toy to share, Bear Junior found something new—a special new Bible. Just then he heard the Bible Amigos say, "Go, go, go!" and they were gone, gone, gone.

Bear Junior waved and whispered, "Thank you. I will share this, too."

Never be afraid to do what God asks, even if you don't want to, or don't understand why. God loves you so much. He will only ask you to do things that will lead you, and those around you, to everlasting joy and peace.

Love,
The Bible Amigos

Edse Walla Donk

The End

*God has more to tell you about this in the Bible;
here are some of our favorite passages:*

Walla's favorite: John 15:10–11

Donk's favorite: John 2:1–11

Edge's favorite: Luke 11:28

Edge's other favorite: Jeremiah 42:3–6